I Spy Nursery Rhymes

Written by Charlotte Raby
and Emily Guille-Marrett
Illustrated by Amanda Enright

Collins

2

3

4

5

6

8

9

12

13

Can you say these nursery rhymes?

 After reading

Letters and Sounds: Phase 1

Word count: 0

Curriculum links: Self-confidence and self-awareness: children are confident to try new activities, and say why they like some activities more than others

Early Learning Goals: Listening and attention: children listen attentively in a range of situations; Understanding: answer 'how' and 'why' questions about their experiences and in response to stories or events.

Developing fluency

- Encourage your child to hold the book and to turn the pages. Look at the pictures together and ask your child how many characters from nursery rhymes they can spot, ensuring they understand which two characters are Jack and Jill. Ask them to choose which nursery rhymes they would like to sing or chant together (e.g. *The Grand Old Duke of York, Mary Mary Quite Contrary*).

- Your child might enjoy you telling them one or more nursery rhymes they don't know, if there are any. If you need to be reminded of the words, try looking them up online or in the Phonics for Letters and Sounds Handbook.

- Ensure your child understands that the book is showing Jack and Jill's journey and that they can spot the two characters on each page.

Phonic practice

- Choose a nursery rhyme from the story, e.g. 'Twinkle, twinkle, little star'. Say it with your child. Ask them if they can point out any of the words that rhyme (e.g. *star and are, high and sky*).

- Can they think of any other words that rhyme with each of the pairs of rhyming words?

- Try this with other nursery rhymes, using pages 14 and 15 for ideas. Draw attention to the rhyming sounds by emphasising the words that rhyme as you say them and point them out if your child is unsure.